IT'S NOT ABOUT THE
BALL!

Veronika Martenova Charles

Illustrated by David Parkins

TUNDRA BOOKS

Published in Canada by Tundra Books, a division of Random House of Canada Limited,
One Toronto Street, Suite 300, Toronto, Ontario M5C 2V6

Published in the United States by Tundra Books of Northern New York,
P.O. Box 1030, Plattsburgh, New York 12901

Library of Congress Control Number: 2012945434

Library and Archives Canada Cataloguing in Publication

Charles, Veronika Martenova
        It's not about the ball! / Veronika Martenova Charles ; illustrated
by David Parkins.

(Easy-to-read wonder tales)
Short stories based on The frog prince tales from around the world.
ISBN 978-1-77049-330-8. – ISBN 978-1-77049-335-3 (EPUB)

        1. Fairy tales. I. Parkins, David II. Title. III. Series: Charles,
Veronika Martenova. Easy-to-read wonder tales.

PS8555.H4224218324 2013   jC813'.54   C2012-905303-1

We acknowledge the financial support of the Government of Canada through the
Canada Book Fund and that of the Government of Ontario through the Ontario Media
Development Corporation's Ontario Book Initiative. We further acknowledge the support of
the Canada Council for the Arts and the Ontario Arts Council for our publishing program.

 ONTARIO ARTS COUNCIL
CONSEIL DES ARTS DE L'ONTARIO

Edited by Stacey Roderick

www.tundrabooks.com

Printed and bound in China

1 2 3 4 5 6   18 17 16 15 14 13

CONTENTS

THE POND
PART 1

"I want to show you something,"

Jake told Lily and Ben

when they came to his house.

He led them to a little pond

in the back of the garden.

"Look over there!" said Jake.

"A frog!" exclaimed Lily.

She took a ball out of her pocket

and dropped it into the water.

"What are you doing?" asked Jake.

"I want to see if the frog will talk,

like in *The Frog Prince*,"

Lily replied.

"There's no ball in the story

I know," said Jake.

"I'll tell it to you."

THE PROMISE

(The Frog Prince from Scotland)

Once there was a queen

who became very sick.

She told her daughter,

"In the courtyard, there is a well

with crystal clear water.

Bring me a drink from it,

and it will heal me."

The princess went to the well,

filled a glass with water,

but saw that it was muddy.

A frog stuck his head out

of the well and said,

"*Ribbit, ribbit!*

If you promise to give me

some food and a bed,

I will give you clear water."

The princess thought to herself,

My mother needs the water,

and this is only a frog.

What does he know of promises?

"Why not?" the princess replied.

"I promise."

She filled the glass again,

and this time the water was clear.

The princess turned around,

leaving the frog by the well,

and returned to the palace.

She gave her mother the water

and thought no more about it.

That evening, the princess heard

croaking at the door.

"Open the door, *ribbit, ribbit!*

It's your promise, keep it, keep it!"

It must be that ugly frog,

thought the princess.

She opened the door a crack,

let the frog in, and went to bed.

But she couldn't sleep

because the frog croaked again,

"Bring me food, *ribbit, ribbit!*

It's your promise, keep it, keep it!"

The princess crawled out of bed
and gave the frog some dinner.
That should keep him quiet,
she thought and went back to bed.

Just as she was falling asleep,

the frog began to croak again,

"Give me a bed, *ribbit, ribbit!*

It's your promise, keep it, keep it!"

"What a pest you are!"

the princess said.

She picked up the slimy frog

and put it at the foot of her bed.

There, the frog croaked again.

"Help me, please, *ribbit, ribbit!*

Get a sword, bring it, bring it!"

Sword! What on earth could I do

with a sword? thought the princess.

"Ribbit, ribbit!"

The frog kept croaking.

I'll never fall asleep with this noise.

I may as well go find a sword.

In the great hall of the castle,

there was an old sword

hanging on the wall.

The princess brought it to her room.

"Now, will you be quiet?"

She climbed back into bed.

After a few seconds,

the frog croaked again.

"Help me, please, *ribbit, ribbit!*

Slice my skin, cut it, cut it!"

"What?" the princess was horrified.

"*Ribbit, ribbit!*"

The frog kept croaking.

Finally, the princess had enough.

She picked up the old sword.

SWOOSH!

The moment the rusty metal

touched the frog's skin,

he changed into

a handsome young man.

"Thank you," he said.

"Keeping your promise freed me

from a wizard's spell.

Please come to my kingdom.

You can be my queen."

"Why not?" said the princess,

and they went to tell her mother.

"The princess cut the frog?"

asked Lily.

"I think so," replied Jake.

"That's how the spell was broken."

"My cousin Jack told me," said Ben,

"that once, at school,

they had to cut a frog."

"That's gross," said Lily.

"I could never do that."

"Do you want to hear another story about a talking frog?" asked Ben.

"Okay," said Jake and Lily.

THE FROG BOY

(*The Frog Prince* from Vietnam)

It happened once

that a woman gave birth

to a frog instead of a baby.

At first, the woman cried,

but then she decided

she would raise the frog

as she would a child.

As the years passed,

the frog grew up

and behaved just like

an ordinary boy.

He followed his mother around

and helped her in the house.

When she was cooking soup,

he hopped up on the stove to stir it,

and if she wasn't looking,

he tasted some with his tongue.

Because the frog was very smart,

his mother decided

he should go to school.

"No!" said the teacher.

"I can't have a frog in the class."

"Please," said the mother,

"he won't cause any trouble."

As the weeks went by,

the frog became the best student.

He learned to write

with a brush in his mouth

and always knew the answers.

In time, the frog finished school.

"I think it is time you find work,"

suggested his mother.

"First, I would like to get married,"

the frog said.

"G-get married?" his mother asked.

"Have you anyone in mind?"

"Yes, Mother," said the frog.

"One of the king's daughters."

The mother was alarmed.

"Son, are you sure?" she asked.

"Tomorrow," the frog told her,

"I will go see the king."

The next morning,

the frog set off for the palace.

He entered the great hall,

hopped in front of the king,

and made his request.

The king burst out laughing.

"Bring my daughters here,"

he ordered his servants.

The king's two daughters entered.

"This frog wants to marry you."

Then the king turned to the frog.

"Which daughter do you like?"

"The one who agrees to marry me,"

the frog replied.

The king became angry.

"Enough joking!"

He turned to his guards.

"Kill this creature!"

"*RIBBIT!*" the frog croaked loudly.

Suddenly, the doors flew open,

and wild beasts burst into the hall.

Elephants charged,

and leopards and tigers growled,

surrounding everybody.

"Have a good day, Your Majesty,"
said the frog as he turned to leave.
"Wait!" the king shouted.
"You can't leave us here
with these beasts."
But the frog kept hopping away.

"What shall we do?"

the king asked his daughters.

"I'd rather be torn by the beasts

than marry that frog,"

shouted the older one.

"I'll marry him," said Tuyen,

her younger sister.

"The frog must be very powerful

but doesn't appear cruel.

Look, all these beasts around us,

yet no one has been harmed."

When she finished speaking,

the animals left the hall.

A few days later,

there was a wedding.

No one dared laugh at the frog

as the tales of his great powers

had spread far.

In the days that followed,

the frog and Tuyen lived happily.

Tuyen found the frog pleasant

and a smart companion.

She grew very fond of him.

Then, one morning,

she found the frog dead

on the pillow beside her.

She lifted him up and cried.

As her tears fell on his body,

she heard someone calling her.

She turned around and

saw a handsome young man.

"How dare you come in here!"

she exclaimed.

"Can't you see

I'm mourning my husband?"

"Tuyen," said the young man,

"I am your husband.

That is only skin you're holding.

A spell turned me into a frog.

Your love turned me

back into a human being."

Tuyen was very happy.

But her sister became jealous.

She hurried to the pond

and chose a frog for herself.

At night, she put it on her pillow,

hoping the frog would change.

But it remained just a frog.

★ ★ ★

"I know why this frog won't talk,"

said Ben.

"It's a girl frog. That's why!"

"That's not it," said Lily.

"I know a story about a girl frog,

and not only could she talk,

but she could sing, too.

I'll tell you the story."

THE SINGING FROG

(*The Frog Prince* from Chile)

There once was a king

who had three sons:

Pablo, Pedro, and Juan.

One day, the king told his sons,

"Go see the world,

find yourself a wife,

and come back in a year."

First, Pablo, the eldest son, left.

After riding for a long time,

he came to a little cottage.

He heard a girl's voice

singing a lovely song.

"Oh, if that girl is single,

I want to marry her," he said.

Her father came to the door.

"Good morning," said Pablo.

"I'd like to meet your daughter."

"Come out, child," called the man.

A frog jumped out of a clay jar.

"This is your daughter?"

asked Pablo in disbelief.

"Yes, she is," the old man replied.

"Forget it," said Pablo.

He pushed the frog with his foot

and rode away.

The next day,

the second brother, Pedro,

set off on the same road.

He, too, stopped at the cottage

when he heard the song.

"I want to marry the girl

who sings so beautifully,"

he said to her father.

"She is not to be married,"

the father told him.

"Let me meet her," Pedro said.

The frog jumped out of the jar.

"You call this your daughter?

What an ugly thing!" cried Pedro,

and he rode away fast.

The following day,

the youngest son, Juan,

set off on the same road.

When he heard the singing,

he said to himself,

This is the girl I want to marry.

The old man came to the door.

"Good morning," said Juan.

"Is that your daughter singing?

I'd like to meet her and

ask her to marry me," said Juan.

"You won't like her looks,"

the father said.

"Looks don't matter to me,"

Juan said.

"I will marry her for her voice.

I give you my word."

"All right," said the father.

"Come out, my child."

The frog jumped out of the jar.

"This is her?" asked Juan.

"Well, I gave you my word

that I'd marry your daughter."

So the next day,

there was a wedding.

But, that night, Juan was sad

that his bride was only a frog.

"Don't be sad," the frog told him.

"I will sing you a lullaby

so you can go to sleep."

And so it went for a year.

When the year was over,

the two older brothers rode by,

returning home with their wives.

They looked inside the cottage

and saw Juan.

"That fool! He married the frog!"

They laughed and rode on.

Juan said to the little frog,

"Today, I was to return home

with my wife

and introduce her to my father.

If I bring you, everyone will laugh."

"Don't worry," said the little frog.

"It will be all right."

So Juan took the little frog,

and they rode to the palace.

At the gate,

the guards stopped them.

"Sorry, Prince," they said.

"This creature can't come inside.

This is not a place for frogs."

Juan picked up the little frog

and held her tight to his heart.

"This is my wife," he said.

"If she can't come in,

then neither can I."

At that moment, the frog trembled

and transformed into a girl

in a beautiful green dress.

"I was enchanted

and turned into a frog," she said.

"Your love changed me back

into a human again."

Juan was overjoyed.

When they entered the palace,

Pablo and Pedro stared at them.

"Where did he find that girl?"

they wondered.

"We thought he married a frog!"

Juan introduced his wife.

"What beauty," said the king.

"Yes, but I have chosen her

for her lovely voice,"

Juan told him.

"Can she sing a song for us?"

asked the king.

The frog girl began to sing,

and everyone fell silent.

"Bravo!" called out the king.

He turned to Juan.

"You have chosen well.

From now on,

it will be you and your wife

who will rule the kingdom."

THE POND
PART 2

Jake's father came out of the house.

"Jake!" he called.

"Why is that ball in the water?

Please don't throw things there."

"Sorry, Dad," Jake said.

"There is a frog in the pond.

We were trying to find out

if it could talk."

"Well, did it talk?" asked his dad.

"Yes," said Jake,

"but only in frog language."

Jake's father laughed and said,

"Don't forget to take out the ball."

"*Ribbit, ribbit*," said Lily.

"What?" asked Jake.

"I said I was sorry

for throwing the ball in."

"*Ribbit, ribbit, ribbit,*"

croaked Ben.

"That meant, let's take

the ball out and play."

"*RIBBIT!*" Jake and Lily agreed.

ABOUT THE STORIES

In the popular version of *The Frog Prince* by the Grimm brothers, a princess drops her golden ball into the water and a frog retrieves it in return for a promise.

The Promise is drawn from several versions of a folktale from Scotland called *The Queen Who Sought a Drink from a Certain Well* ("*Wearie Well at the Warldis End*") that can be traced back to 1548. Similar versions of the story were also found in Germany.

The Frog Boy is based on a story called *Master Frog* that comes from Vietnam.

The Singing Frog was inspired by *Little Frog*, a South American fairy tale from Chile.